The Adventure Continues . . .

Hi! I'm Jackie. I'm an archaeologist. I study ancient treasures to learn about the past.

Legend says that twelve talismans are scattered around the world. Each one has a picture of an animal on it. And each holds a different kind of magic.

I discovered the first one, a rooster talisman, in the center of a golden shield in Germany. Since then I have found eleven of the twelve. But an evil group called The Dark Hand has captured two of them. And if they can get all twelve talismans, they will rule the world.

There is only one talisman left to find—the tiger. And I've heard it's in a very strange place—inside a blueberry pie at a county fair.

Time to chow down!

A PARACHUTE PRESS BOOK

TM and © 2003 Adelaide Productions, Inc. All Rights Reserved.

Published by Grosset & Dunlap, a division of Penguin Putnam Books for Young Readers, New York. GROSSET & DUNLAP is a trademark of Penguin Putnam, Inc. Published simultaneously in Canada. Printed in U.S.A.

Library of Congress Cataloging-in-Publication Data is available.

ISBN 0-448-43123-8
A B C D E F G H I J

JACKIE CHAN
ADVENTURES ™

Day of
the Dragon

A novelization by Eliza Willard
based on the teleplays "The Tiger and the Pussycat"
by David Slack and "Day of the Dragon" by Alexx Van Dyne

Grosset & Dunlap

"I know the tiger talisman is in one of these blueberry pies," Jackie Chan whispered to his niece, Jade. "We just have to find it."

The pies were lined up on a long table at a county fair. A pie-eating contest was about to begin. Jackie was poking the pies with a fork, hoping to find the talisman.

"Piece of cake—um, I mean, pie!" Jade said. "We're signed up for the contest. We'll just eat until we find the talisman!"

Jackie kept poking. He knew Jade was right. But if he could find the talisman before the contest began, he wouldn't have to eat all that pie!

"It's a good thing that farmer over there is our only competition," Jade added. She nodded toward a skinny old man in overalls at the end of the table.

He gave them a toothless grin, then popped a set of false teeth into his mouth.

Then Jackie spotted something huge coming their way. A mountain of a man with a stomach to match. Tohru.

He was The Dark Hand's mightiest

enforcer. The Dark Hand was an evil group on a mission to find all twelve magic talismans. They wanted to use the power of the talismans to rule the world!

"Looks like someone else is joining the contest," Jackie mumbled.

Tohru sat down at the table, ready to eat. Jackie and Jade took their seats.

"Maybe Tohru didn't leave room for dessert," Jade wished out loud.

Jackie shook his head. Tohru was so big, he had room for ten dinners and ten desserts.

The referee blew his whistle. The contest began.

Jade chomped away as fast as she could.

Tohru swallowed each pie whole. He checked for the talisman with his tongue.

The skinny old man sat in front of one pie and slowly picked through it with a fork.

Jackie didn't bother eating. He dug through the pies with his hands, searching for the talisman.

Suddenly, he heard a crunch. The others heard it, too. Everyone stared at the old farmer.

The man reached into his mouth. Out came the farmer's false teeth—with a small, eight-sided stone stuck between them.

It was the tiger talisman!

"There's something crunchy in my pie," the farmer complained.

Jackie leaped onto the table. He snatched the talisman away, false teeth and all!

"I'm sorry!" he shouted to the old man. "I'll bring back your teeth—I promise! Thank you!"

But before Jackie had a chance to jump off the table, Tohru slammed his foot on it.

Bang! The table tilted, and Jackie lost his balance. He slid down the table—right into Tohru's arms.

Tohru lifted Jackie by the collar. "Give me the—"

Splat! Before Tohru could finish, Jade slammed a pie into his face. He dropped Jackie.

Jade grinned at Jackie. "He was going to say 'Give me that pie,' right?"

she joked. "Well, I gave it to him."

Jackie picked up Jade and dashed away. He glanced back to see Tohru wiping pie out of his eyes.

A bell rang, and the referee pinned a blue medal on Tohru's chest. "Forty-seven pies!" the referee cheered. "We have a winner—and a new record!"

Tohru frowned.

Jackie chuckled and disappeared from the fair with Jade—and the tiger talisman.

"After nine centuries, all twelve talismans have been found," Shendu growled in his low voice. His red eyes glowed in the smoky lair of The Dark Hand. "Yet I have only *two!* While Jackie Chan has *ten!* You and your enforcers have failed me again, Valmont!"

Tohru trembled with fear. He had just returned from the pie-eating contest without the tiger talisman, and Shendu was furious.

Tohru's boss, Valmont, played nervously with his cane. He was the leader of The Dark Hand, but he was afraid of Shendu, too.

Shendu was an evil spirit trapped inside a stone statue of a dragon. Twelve slots dotted the statue—one slot for each talisman. Shendu wanted to come alive again and rule the Earth. But he couldn't do it without all twelve talismans.

"Don't worry, Shendu—" Valmont began.

"The Chinese New Year approaches," Shendu said. "I *must* have all twelve talismans before then—if you ever wish to see the lost treasure."

Valmont's lips twitched with rage. Shendu had promised to share his treasure with Valmont—*if* Valmont brought him the talismans.

"The talismans are locked away in Section Thirteen," Valmont said. Section Thirteen was a top secret crime-fighting group. Its location was top secret, too. The leader of Section Thirteen, Captain Augustus Black, was a friend of Jackie's.

"But, I'm sure Jackie Chan will tell us where Section Thirteen is," Valmont said. "With proper *prodding* . . ."

He pulled an electric dagger out of

the top of his cane. It buzzed with power.

"Find him," Shendu ordered. *"Now."*

"Tohru!" Valmont shook his cane at the giant. "Bring me Jackie Chan."

Chapter 2

Jade crept into the kitchen in the back of Uncle's antique shop in San Francisco. "Chinese New Year rocks!" she whispered to herself. "Especially the sweets." She reached into a basket of candy.

"Jade . . ." Jackie warned. "It's two more days until the New Year."

Rats! Jackie had spotted her. He and Uncle were in the library studying a bunch of dusty old books. They were trying to find out about the tiger talisman.

"Aw," Jade complained. She put back the candy.

"Hot-cha!" Uncle shouted, thumping a book. "Here it is. The tiger talisman has the power of *balance*."

Jade dashed into the library and snatched the talisman from Uncle's hand. She leaped on top of a teetering stack of books and tried to balance on one leg.

"Cool!" she cried. "So whoever has the talisman can't lose her balance. Whoa!" She tumbled off the stack of books.

Jackie caught her just in time. "Not *that* kind of balance," he said. "The kind of balance your parents in Hong

Kong sent you here to learn."

"Oh," Jade said. She gave the tiger talisman back to Uncle. *That* kind of balance was no fun at all.

Uncle pointed to the design on the talisman. It showed two tigers. Each chased the other's tail.

"Within every one of us are opposite forces," Uncle explained. "Light and dark, good and evil. The Chinese call it yin and yang."

"Yeah, right," Jade joked. "Like Jackie has a dark side."

"I do," Jackie said. "Her name is Jade."

"Very funny," Jade said. "What's the big deal about balance? It's not even a real power."

"Good," Jackie said. "I will enjoy

taking this powerless talisman to Section Thirteen so we can put this quest to rest."

"While Jade will enjoy making tea for dear old Uncle," Uncle added.

"Yes, Uncle," Jade said. But making tea wasn't her idea of fun. Now that the search for the talismans was over, things were going to be pretty dull around here, she thought.

Jackie flipped the talisman in his hand as he headed out of Uncle's shop. When he caught it, he spotted something he hadn't noticed before. A very thin crack ran down the middle of the talisman.

Jackie remembered the farmer at the pie-eating contest. He had bitten the talisman with his false teeth. That must have cracked it!

Snap! The talisman broke in half. A blinding white light flashed at Jackie.

"Whoa!" Jackie cried. He floated up into the air—and split into two Jackies!

He landed on the floor and stared at his other self. It was like looking into a mirror! Jackie held half the talisman in one hand. His double had the other half.

"This is awful!" Jackie cried. What was going on?

The other Jackie cracked his neck—*crack! crack!*—then headed into the kitchen, straight for the basket of candy.

Jackie followed his double. *Crunch.*

Oh, no! He'd stepped on something. He lifted his shoe. A bug!

He ran into the library. "Uncle!" he sobbed. "I stepped on a bug!"

"Huh?" Uncle was confused. "What are you talking about?"

"A bug!" Jackie wailed. "I killed a bug!"

Jade went into the kitchen to fix tea for Uncle. There stood Jackie— eating her New Year's candy!

"Mmm, good," Jackie said. He smacked his lips.

"Hey!" Jade shouted. "That's my candy!"

"Not anymore," Jackie said. He opened up the refrigerator. "Got milk?"

Jade couldn't believe it. Jackie had eaten all of her Chinese New Year candy. And she didn't even get one piece! She started for the library. Jackie was acting weird. Maybe Uncle could straighten him out.

Uncle met her in the dining room. "What happened to Jackie?" he asked Jade. "He is such a crybaby!"

"No way. He's such a jerk!" Jade corrected him.

"He's in the library, weeping all over my research!" Uncle complained.

Jade glanced at Uncle. "No, he's in the kitchen, raiding the fridge."

"How could Jackie be in the study and in the kitchen at the same time?" Uncle asked. "Jackie!" he called.

One Jackie stepped out of the

study, wiping tears from his eyes. Another one came from the kitchen. He was drinking milk right out of the container. He burped.

Whoa, Jade thought. *Two* Jackies? What's going on?

Chapter 3

Jade noticed the broken talisman halves in the hands of the two Jackies. "Uncle, look!"

Uncle gasped. He hurried into his study and opened a book.

Jade and the two Jackies followed behind him.

"The talisman broke in half," Uncle told Jade. "That made Jackie's yin separate from his yang. One of these Jackies is his good side. The other is his bad side," he said.

"Whoa," Jade said. "Jackie Light and Jackie Dark."

Uncle nodded.

"I am the dark side!" the weeping Jackie cried out. "I murdered a poor little bug. It never did anything to me!" He burst into tears again.

The other Jackie rolled his eyes. "Give me a break," he said.

Jade pointed at him. "You're the one who ate my candy!" she shouted. "You're evil. Evil!"

Jackie Dark shrugged.

"He is not evil," Uncle explained. "Without his good side to guide him, he lacks sound judgment. They must join the two halves of the talisman together. That is the only way they can become one Jackie again."

Jackie Dark frowned. "I don't want to be with that wimp."

"I can't be with him!" Jackie Light agreed. "He burps out loud—without saying 'Excuse me'!"

"You must restore the balance!" Uncle insisted. *Thwap!* He rapped both Jackies on the head.

"Ow!" Jackie Light cried.

But Jackie Dark thwapped Uncle back!

"You will pay for that!" Uncle shouted. He thwapped Jackie Dark again. Jackie Dark rapped him back. *Thwap! Thwap! Thwap!*

Through the shop window, Jade spotted two long black cars pulling up to the curb. Big, burly men piled out of the cars and into the street.

"Uh, Jackies?" Jade said. "We've got trouble."

Uncle and Jackie Dark stopped thwapping each other.

Outside the shop, a small army of thugs gathered.

"Oh, no!" both Jackies gasped at once. "The Dark Hand!"

"We must hide the talisman," Uncle whispered.

Jade, Uncle, and the two Jackies huddled in the dining room. Each Jackie slipped his half of the talisman into his pocket.

"What are we going to do?" Jade asked.

Jackie Dark made a fist. "We're going to make them scream and

21

yell for mercy," he growled.

But Jackie Light looked scared. "Run!" he cried. He grabbed Jade and added, "This is no place for children!" He scurried out of the room with Jade under his arm.

Bam! The front door of the shop burst open. In stepped a group of The Dark Hand enforcers. They were led by Finn, Chow, and Tohru.

"Jackie Chan," Tohru said. "You're coming with—"

Before he could finish, Jackie Dark flew through the air and kicked Tohru in the chest.

The giant crashed to the floor. He was out cold!

The other enforcers stared at Jackie. They had never seen him act that way before. Normally, Jackie did not fight unless he had to.

"You didn't even let him finish," Finn protested.

Jackie Dark cracked his neck. *Crack! Crack!* Then he glared at the other enforcers

"Who's next?" he asked.

Jackie Light dragged Jade out to the back alley. But another group of Dark Hand enforcers were waiting for him.

"Whoa!" Jackie Light cried. He shoved Jade back into the kitchen. She'd be safe there.

Jade peeked through the door.

The enforcers moved in on Jackie Light. He held up one finger and said, "Remember, the greatest victory is the battle not fought!"

Jade covered her eyes. "Oh, no," she moaned. "Jackie Light's gonna get creamed!"

Ratso, a member of The Dark hand stood in front of the enforcers. "Get him!" he shouted.

Jackie Light back-flipped onto a Dumpster and scrambled over a fence. The Dark Hand enforcers hurried after him.

Jackie Light may be packing Jackie's moves, Jade thought, but he's still a big chicken! He's going to need some 'Jade Dark' to balance him out.

She followed Jackie Light and the enforcers across a rooftop and into the street.

Meanwhile, Jackie Dark quickly took care of the other enforcers. Within minutes he threw them all out onto the street. They piled on top of each other, groaning.

"Seems like Chan's in a bad mood today," Finn said.

Chow straightened his sunglasses. "He's a psycho! He stole my leather jacket!"

"Who cares?" Finn said. "Look what *I* got." He held up half of the tiger talisman.

Chow smiled. But then a shadow loomed over them. It was Jackie Dark. And he was wearing Chow's leather jacket.

Finn and Chow backed away, scared.

Jackie Dark plucked Chow's sunglasses off his face. He put them on. With the glasses and the jacket, he looked tougher than ever.

"Let's get out of here!" Finn screamed. He and Chow and the other enforcers raced to their cars and peeled away.

Jackie Dark tore after them, but the cars were too fast. He scrambled up to the top of a hill and watched the cars wind down the road.

A delivery truck zipped by, carrying a load of fish. Jackie Dark jumped onto the back and clung to the bumper. Soon the truck cut in front of The Dark Hand's cars.

"It's him!" Chow yelled. "What's he going to do to us?"

Jackie Dark opened the back door of the truck. Fish poured out and covered the car behind it. There was so much fish, the driver couldn't see through the windshield!

The thugs jumped out of the car and tried to run away. But they slipped and skidded over the fish.

Jackie Dark grabbed Finn.

Finn held up the talisman half. "Here!" he cried. "Take it!"

Jackie Dark cracked his neck. "What, and spoil my fun?" Jackie Dark was about to punch Finn. Then a giant hand tapped him on the shoulder.

"This better be good," Jackie Dark murmured. He turned around.

Whap! Tohru swung a huge fish

like a baseball bat. He hit Jackie Dark
with it.

Jackie Dark fell to the ground.
Everything went black.

Chapter 4

Jackie Light dashed through the streets of Chinatown. The enforcers were fast on his heels. And Jade was right behind them.

A New Year's parade was marching down the street. Crowds cheered. A long paper dragon danced in the street. Jackie Light ducked into the parade.

"Hey!" Finn shouted. "Where did he go?"

The enforcers looked around. So did Jade. No sign of Jackie.

Ratso pointed down an alley. "Maybe he went that way," he said.

Jade began to follow them. But then she noticed something under the dancing dragon. A familiar pair of shoes. Jackie's shoes!

Jade peeked under the dragon. "Hey, Jackie," she said. "The coast is clear. They're gone."

Jackie popped out from under the costume. "Thank goodness," he said. "I didn't want to have to hurt them."

Jade rolled her eyes. Jackie Light was such a wimp. "I wonder what happened to Jackie Dark," she said.

They climbed a steep hill. From there they could see the whole neighborhood. Jade and Jackie Light scanned the streets.

"Jackie! Look!" Jade cried.

Far below, at the foot of the hill, was Jackie Dark. He had been knocked out. And the enforcers were stuffing him into their car!

Tohru and the enforcers brought Jackie Dark to Valmont. Finn gave Valmont the half talisman.

"Half a talisman?" Valmont frowned. "It's a start, I suppose." He dropped it into his shirt pocket.

Chow tied Jackie Dark to a chair in an empty gray room. Finn waved an electric sword near his head.

"Tell me where Section Thirteen is," Valmont demanded. "Or else!"

Finn waved the sword closer and closer to Jackie Dark's face. But Jackie Dark stayed cool. He still wore Chow's sunglasses and leather jacket.

Then Valmont's video phone rang.

Valmont clicked it on. "What is it?" he snapped.

Ratso's face appeared on the video screen. "We just lost Jackie Chan," he told Valmont. "We almost had him!"

"What are you talking about?" Valmont said. "He's right here!"

"He can't be," Ratso insisted. "He just got away from us a minute ago!"

Valmont's eyes grew wide with surprise. He glanced at Jackie in the chair. Ratso could be stupid, but he wasn't *that* stupid. What was going on?

"Come back to headquarters,"

Valmont ordered Ratso. Then he hurried into Shendu's lair.

Shendu's eyes glowed when Valmont told him about the two Jackies. "Chan must have divided the tiger talisman in two," Shendu explained. "Now *he* is divided—into light and dark."

"So which Chan do we have?" Valmont wondered. He went back to the gray room. Finn and Chow were supposed to be guarding Jackie Dark. But the three of them were laughing together like old friends.

"You know, Chan," Finn said, "you're a pretty cool guy."

"Yeah," Chow agreed. "Too bad we have to get rid of you."

Hmm, Valmont thought. This must

be Jackie's dark side. Maybe Jackie Dark is not our enemy after all. Maybe he is on *our* side.

"Perhaps we do not have to get rid of you, Chan," Valmont said. "There might be another option. Bring me the talismans from Section Thirteen, and I'll make you rich."

Jackie Dark shrugged. "Works for me," he said.

Chapter 5

"Captain Black doesn't believe in magic," Jade said to Jackie Light. "He'll never believe there are two Jackies."

They stood outside a red phone booth—the secret entrance to Section Thirteen. Jade knew they would need Captain Black's help to free Jackie Dark.

"I have to tell him that Jackie Dark was captured," Jade said. "But if he sees you, he'll think it's a joke. So you have to wait here. Okay, Jackie?"

Jackie Light nodded.

"Good," Jade said. "Now give me your half of the talisman. I'll put it into the vault for safekeeping."

Jackie Light gave Jade his talisman half. Then she stepped into the phone booth, which was really an elevator, and *whooshed* down to Section Thirteen.

She hurried to Captain Black's office. "Captain Black!" she cried. "The Dark Hand captured Jackie!"

Captain Black sprang to his feet. "What? How did they—"

Just then he saw Jackie slip down the hallway. Jackie was wearing a black leather jacket and carrying a red fishing box. Captain Black relaxed.

"You almost fooled me," he told Jade. "I just saw Jackie in the hall."

Jade whirled around. But by then Jackie was gone.

"I'm serious!" Jade said. "Jackie is in trouble. You've got to believe me!"

Captain Black turned back to his work. "Now, now, Jade." Through the door, he saw Jackie walk by again.

"Look," he said. "There he goes again."

Jade turned around. This time she caught sight of Jackie as he passed. "Whoops," she said.

Jade had told Jackie to stay outside. Why hadn't he listened? She ran out of the office and chased Jackie down the hall. She caught up with him as he waited for the elevator.

"You totally blew it!" she yelled at him. "I told you to wait outside!"

She noticed his leather jacket. Was he wearing that before? And why was he carrying a red fishing box?

"Cool jacket," she said, touching the leather.

"Get your hands off it!" Jackie snapped. The elevator door opened. Jackie got in. The door closed before Jade could follow him.

"Hey!" Jade shouted. She pounded on the door. "Why are you being such a jerk?"

And then it hit her.

That wasn't Jackie Light! That was Jackie Dark!

Where is Jade? Jackie Light wondered, as he waited on the street. What is taking her so long?

Whoosh! Someone appeared in the red phone booth. That must be Jade now, Jackie Light thought.

But it wasn't Jade. It was Jackie Dark.

"Brother!" Jackie Light cheered. "You're okay!" He glanced at the red metal box Jackie Dark carried. "Are you going fishing?"

Jackie Dark shook the box. The talismans rattled inside.

"I *went* fishing," he said. "Talisman fishing."

Jackie Light gasped. Jackie Dark had stolen the talismans! "You're a bad boy," he scolded.

"And you're ugly!" Jackie Dark shot back. "Now, where's the other half of the tiger?" He searched Jackie Light's pockets.

Jackie Light giggled. "That tickles," he said.

Jackie Dark couldn't find the other half of the talisman. So he shoved Jackie Light into the phone booth. *Whoosh!* Down he went.

The elevator door opened. Jackie Light spilled out into Section Thirteen. He landed at Jade's feet.

Jade grabbed him by the collar. "Okay, meanie!" she shouted. "What are you—"

"Was I mean to you?" Jackie Light said. "I'm sorry!"

Jade blinked. This Jackie was nice—and he wasn't wearing a leather jacket. It had to be Jackie Light!

"What are you doing down here?" she asked. "I told you to wait outside."

"The bad me stole the talismans!" Jackie Light explained.

Jade gasped. "So that's what he was doing here!" She held up the half talisman. "Well, he still doesn't have *all* of them." She stuck the half talisman inside her sneaker for safekeeping. "You've got to stop him!"

"I tried scolding him," Jackie Light said. "But it didn't work."

"Of course it didn't work!" Jade snapped. "I mean *stop* him, Jackie-style." She jumped into a kung fu stance.

41

"Oh, no, no, no!" Jackie Light cried. "Chop-socky solves nothing!"

Jade groaned in frustration. "I guess I'll have to stop him myself," she said.

She got into the elevator and hurried outside. She spotted Jackie Dark as he put on his sunglasses and turned a corner. Jade followed him through an alley to a run-down part of town.

"Wait!" Jade shouted. She ran up to Jackie Dark and grabbed the red metal box. "You can't do this. If The Dark Hand gets all the talismans, something really bad will happen!"

"So?" Jackie Dark snatched the box away from her.

"But you're not evil, remember?"

Jade pleaded. "Uncle said *everyone* has yin and yang—and you can't be *all* yang!"

Jackie Dark pushed past her. "Yang-dang-doodle dooby-do," he sang.

Jade stopped and watched him walk away. She couldn't believe it. How could Jackie—*her* Jackie—do this?

She took a deep breath. She didn't want to hurt him. But she knew she had to stop him somehow.

"Yeeeahhh!" Jade cried as she ran after him.

"Huh?" Jackie Dark turned.

Jade leaped—and kicked him right in the sunglasses.

The sunglasses cracked. Jade tumbled to the ground.

Jackie Dark glared at her. His sunglasses were broken. He pulled them off and dropped them on the ground.

"I *liked* those," he growled.

Jackie dropped the red metal box. Then he cracked his neck—*crack! crack!*

Jade cowered on the ground. Jackie Dark had never looked meaner.

"Oopsy?" she whispered.

With a terrible roar, Jackie Dark took a flying leap—and aimed a deadly kick at Jade!

Chapter 6

"Jackie, no!" Jade shouted. She shut her eyes and waited to feel Jackie Dark's foot hit her.

But nothing happened. She peeked through her hands.

Wham! Someone knocked Jackie Dark aside. He tumbled to the ground. Jade looked up to see who had saved her.

Jackie Light!

"It's not nice to drop-kick little

girls," Jackie Light said, frowning.

"See what I mean?" Jade said to Jackie Dark. "If Jackie Light has a fighting side, then you must have a nice side."

Jackie Dark rose to his feet. He stepped toward the metal box of talismans that sat on the ground. "As soon as I give the talismans to Valmont, I'll have a *rich* side," he told Jade.

"You can't do that!" Jade rushed to the box. She picked it up and hid behind Jackie Light.

"Give me that box, you little gnat!" Jackie Dark snarled.

"Name-calling is not nice either!" Jackie Light scolded.

Jackie Dark cracked his neck. Then

he threw a kick at Jackie Light. *Pow! Pow! Pow!*

But Jackie Light gracefully dodged his kicks and punches.

Jade moved away and knelt in front of the box. Jackie Light might need a little backup, she thought. I bet the powers of the talismans could help him.

Then a large dark shadow loomed over her. She looked up and gasped. It was Tohru!

Jade clutched the box. "These are *not* the talismans!" she cried.

But Tohru didn't believe her. He grabbed the box.

Jade held on to the box with all her might.

Tohru just carried off the box with

Jade clinging to it.

"Jackie!" she screamed. "Help!"

Both Jackies stopped fighting— just in time to see Tohru toss Jade and the talismans into the back of a car. The car drove away.

"Jade!" Jackie Light called.

"I kind of liked her," Jackie Dark admitted. "She's scrappy."

"She's family!" Jackie Light cried. "We have to save her!"

Jackie Dark seemed surprised. "Really? We do?"

"Come help me," Jackie Light said. "You'll get to fight more guys. . . ."

Jackie Dark couldn't resist a fight. "Let's go," he said.

"Eight, nine, ten . . ." Valmont

counted. He carefully placed each of the talismans into its slot in Shendu's statue.

Jade watched from across the room. She was trapped in The Dark Hand's headquarters, in a skyscraper high above ground. She was handcuffed to a chair. Tohru guarded her.

". . . and eleven," Valmont finished.

Shendu's red eyes glowed with pleasure. "Yes," he hissed. "I can feel my power coming back."

Jade was amazed. "The statue talks!" she cried. "You guys are working for a statue?"

Tohru glared at her. "Quiet!"

Valmont pulled half of the tiger talisman from his pocket. "Eleven and a half . . ." he counted.

He turned to Tohru and held out a hand.

Tohru blinked. "What?"

"Where is the other half of the talisman?" Valmont shouted.

Jade could feel the half talisman in her shoe. She shifted, trying to hide her foot.

"I do not have it," Tohru said. "Why do you always blame me?"

"Maybe Chan has it," Valmont said. Then his eyes fell on Jade. "Or maybe . . ."

Uh-oh, Jade thought.

Valmont pounced on Jade. He searched her for the half talisman.

Jade would not give in without a fight. She squirmed and kicked Valmont as hard as she could. But she couldn't escape. She was still hand-cuffed to the chair.

Suddenly, the doors burst open. *Pow!* In came Jackie Dark and Jackie Light!

"The Jackies!" Jade cheered. "I knew Jackie Dark couldn't be all bad."

"Get them!" Valmont ordered.

Ratso, Finn, Chow, and Tohru attacked Jackie Dark and Jackie Light. But with their kung fu moves, the two Jackies quickly knocked out the enforcers.

"I apologize!" Jackie Light cried.

"Jackie, help!" Jade screamed.

Jackie Dark pushed Valmont aside.

Valmont flew through the air and landed on the floor. He sat up. One of Jade's shoes had come off in his hand.

He turned it over. The half talisman dropped into his lap.

Jackie Light snapped open Jade's handcuffs. "Are you okay?" he asked her.

Jade pointed at Valmont. He was walking toward Shendu with the half talisman in his hand.

"Stop him!" Jade yelled. "He has all twelve talismans!"

"No!" the Jackies shouted. They leaped across the room to stop Valmont.

But it was too late.

Valmont snapped the talisman half into the slot, next to its mate.

The two halves fused together. A blinding white light flashed out of the tiger talisman.

Jackie Light and Jackie Dark jumped into the air to kick Valmont. But the flash of light caught them. It held them up in the air.

Then Jackie Light and Jackie Dark fused together, just like the talisman. They became one person again.

Jackie tumbled to the floor in front of Shendu. He sat up and patted his chest. He was himself again—one whole Jackie Chan!

"Game over, Chan," Valmont said. "*Way* over."

Jackie stared at the dragon statue. Swirls of ghostly energy surrounded it. One by one, the talismans glowed with light.

Then the statue began to stretch and move. And one by one talismans were sucked into its body. Fire poured out of the statue's mouth. The statue came alive! It morphed into a gigantic dragon.

"I *live!*" the dragon roared.

Chapter 7

"I was trapped inside that statue for nine hundred years," Shendu growled. "But now I live again! And the world is mine!"

Jackie and Jade huddled together, shaking. Shendu was the most horrible creature they had ever seen!

He was as tall as a house, with sharp white fangs and long ugly claws. Huge muscles rippled under his scaly green skin. His glowing red eyes sent out blinding hot laser beams. He was a total monster!

Valmont watched the dragon, looking pleased.

"At long last," Shendu said. "My powers are restored. I have heat-beam eyes!" He turned toward Jade.

"Get down!" Jackie shouted. He shoved Jade out of the way.

Shendu shot a flaming red beam at them. It just missed Jackie. It hit the floor, burning a hole in it.

"And my favorite power," Shendu added. "Combustion!"

A blast from the monster's claws shot across the room at Jackie.

Jackie dodged it. The blast blew a huge hole through the wall—and blew Jackie right out of the twenty-story building.

"Aaaaugh!" Jackie screamed. He fell down, down, down through the air.

He spotted a long rope running along the outside of the building. He reached and grabbed it. He slid down the rope and landed on a window-washer's rig.

"Whoa!" the window-washer cried.

"Jackie!" Up in Shendu's lair, Jade ran to the huge hole in the wall. She stared down at Jackie.

The charred floor under Jade's feet began to give way. It crumbled—and Jade fell out of the skyscraper, too!

"Jackieeee!" she screamed.

Jackie looked up. Jade was falling through the air. He had to catch her—quick!

"Grab my legs!" he told the window-washer.

The window-washer grabbed Jackie's ankles.

Jackie leaped off the rig, reaching for Jade. *Whump!* He caught her by one wrist.

Jade and Jackie dangled off the window-washer's rig, ten stories above the ground.

The window-washer hauled them up to safety. Jade and Jackie stood on his rig, catching their breath.

Jackie pulled out his cell phone and called Captain Black.

"Captain Black, this is urgent," Jackie said. "We're going to need everything Section Thirteen has to destroy a giant dra—"

Jade snatched the phone away from him. She knew that Captain Black would never believe in a giant dragon.

"To fight Valmont," she said into the phone. "He's large and in charge. Come quick!" She clicked off the phone.

"Thank you," Jackie said. He leaped up and grabbed the rope that held the rig. "I'm going to climb back up there," he said. "You two ride this thing down to the bottom. *Both* of you."

Jade pouted. She hated it when Jackie left her out of the action.

Jackie climbed up the rope, all the way to the top of the building. He peered through the giant hole he had fallen through.

A broken electrical cable shot out sparks. Tohru and the enforcers stirred on the floor. The blast had knocked them out, but they were starting to wake up.

"Whoa, Shen-dude," Finn said when he saw the giant dragon. "Welcome back to life."

"Yeah," Ratso agreed. "It's good to see you up and around."

Valmont picked up his cane. He pointed to the damage around the room.

"Well, the office is a mess," he said to Shendu. "But my share of the lost treasure should more than cover the damages."

"Oh, yes, that," Shendu growled. "I'm sorry, Valmont. But you did not bring the talismans to me. Jackie Chan did."

Valmont gasped. "But, Shendu— that's just one tiny little detail—" he sputtered.

Shendu put his huge face close to Valmont's.

Valmont shrank back.

"Read my lips," Shendu said. "Our deal is off. I will not share the lost treasure with you."

Valmont shook with fear. He backed up toward his enforcers.

"Tohru," he ordered. "Make this deadbeat pay up."

Tohru stared at the gigantic monster. Tohru was as big as ten men put together, but Shendu was bigger than twenty.

61

Finn patted Tohru on the back. "You go, bro. We're right behind you—in spirit."

Tohru trembled. "But, master . . ." he began.

Valmont gritted his teeth. "Do it!" he cried.

Shaking, Tohru stepped toward Shendu. Then, like magic, Tohru rose up off the ground. He floated in midair.

"Do not forget," Shendu warned Tohru. "I have the power of levitation." Shendu lifted a tremendous arm. "And super-strength!"

With his thumb and forefinger, Shendu gave Tohru a dainty flick. Tohru shot through the air like a bullet.

"Ugh!" Tohru grunted. He crashed

right through the office doors. His body flew down the hall, smashed through the elevator, then burst through the wall of the skyscraper! He flew out of the building and landed on the roof of a structure below.

Valmont and the enforcers gasped. They stared through the Tohru-shaped hole in the wall.

"All right, Shendu," Valmont agreed, shaking. "The treasure is yours."

"Of course it is," Shendu said. "I'll have it once I reclaim my kingdom. Which will happen soon. Very soon."

Jackie climbed into the room. "I hate to spoil your wonderful plan," he said. He grabbed the sparking electrical cable and hurled it at Shendu.

A huge shock jolted the monster. "Aaaarg!" he roared. Then he shook off the electricity.

Jackie stared at the dragon. He wasn't hurt at all!

"You fool!" Shendu shouted. "The dog talisman makes me immortal! I cannot be killed!"

"This is our cue to leave, gentlemen," Valmont said. He and The Dark Hand enforcers slipped out of the room.

Jackie knew they wouldn't get far. Jade and Captain Black would be waiting for them downstairs.

"Who—or what—are you?" Jackie asked the dragon.

Shendu's eyes burned red. "I am the Keeper of the Talismans," he growled. "I am the One Who Brings Doom. And I am the one who does away with you—for once and for all!"

Shendu drew himself up to his full height. His whole body glowed. He aimed—and shot a massive fireball right at Jackie!

Chapter 8

The fireball roared across the room.

"Aaaaagh!" Jackie shouted, running for his life. He raced down the hall. The fireball chased him. It burned the backs of his shoes.

Jackie reached the Tohru-shaped hole in the elevator. There was only one way to go: down.

Jackie dived down the elevator shaft. The fireball shot past him. It disappeared though the hole Tohru had made in the wall of the building.

Jackie clung to an elevator cable. Phew, he thought. That was close!

He climbed back up to the top floor—just in time. The elevator shot up. The doors opened. Jade and Captain Black stepped out.

Jackie put a finger to his lips. "Shh!" he whispered. "Follow me." He led them down the scorched hallway.

They crept toward The Dark Hand's lair. Jackie wanted Captain Black to see the monster for himself. Now he'd have to believe them!

They peeked into the lair. Shendu was perched near the hole he had blown through the wall. He didn't notice them. Then he jumped.

Whoosh! The giant dragon flew

through the air like a supersonic jet. He darted among the tall buildings and disappeared.

Captain Black turned to Jackie, stunned. "Jackie, what was that thing?"

"A demon," Jackie said. "He just used the power of the levitation talisman and the speed talisman. They helped him to fly."

Captain Black stared at Jackie. "No. Really," he said. "What was it?"

Jade shrugged. "It used to be a statue."

"We've got Valmont and his men behind bars at Section Thirteen," Captain Black said. "I'll question them and—"

"They won't tell you anything," Jackie said. "They want the demon's treasure." He paused, thinking.

"The Section Thirteen manual doesn't cover demons," Jackie said. "I think we should call in an expert."

Captain Black raised an eyebrow. "You can't mean . . ."

Jade nodded. "Jackie's right. We need Uncle."

"And then the demon said he was going to 'reclaim his kingdom,'" Jackie told Uncle.

They were gathered in Uncle's shop. Uncle was listening as Jackie, Jade, and Captain Black told him what had happened.

"Hmm, I see," Uncle said. "What did this demon look like, *exactly?*"

Captain Black rolled his eyes. It

was hard for him to be patient with Uncle. "Fifteen feet tall, red eyes, big claws and teeth. That isn't exact enough for you?"

Uncle glared at Captain Black. "Thousands of demons have lived throughout history. I need more information. A symbol, a name— anything."

"Chan!" a voice boomed from behind them.

Jackie turned to see Tohru in the doorway. He had a bandage on his head, a cast on his leg, and one arm in a sling. He had been hurt when he fell out of The Dark Hand's head-quarters. But he was still alive.

Jackie tensed, but Tohru didn't look so tough now. "Go away!" Jackie shouted. "We have no more talismans!"

Tohru took a step forward. "I did not come to fight. I came to help."

"How can you help us?" Jade asked.

"I can answer your uncle's question," Tohru said.

Everyone stared at Tohru. Did he really want to help?

"The demon's name is Shendu," Tohru offered.

"Thank you, Tohru," Uncle said. He reached for one of his old, old books. "That's all I need to know."

Uncle opened the dusty book. Everyone gathered around.

"Here it is." Uncle pointed to a page in the book. "Shendu. He was the evil warlord of a huge kingdom. His subjects rose up against him.

They put him in prison. The twelve talismans—the source of his power—were scattered to the winds."

"Now he has the talismans—and his power back," Jackie said. "But what does he want? What will he do?"

Uncle turned a page in the book. "Shendu vowed to return to his kingdom," he explained. "His palace will rise from its ashes. And he will open a portal—a door to another world. Hundreds of fire-breathing dragons will pour out of the portal."

"Dragons?" Captain Black repeated. "Why?"

"They are his army," Uncle said. "He will get revenge on his people—the great-great-great-great-great-grandchildren of those who betrayed him!"

Uncle paused. Then his eyes got wide. "This means he will destroy all of Asia!"

Jade gasped. She knew two very special people in Asia. "Oh, no!" she cried. "Mom and Dad!"

73

Jackie put an arm around Jade to comfort her. Jade's parents lived in Hong Kong. If Shendu destroyed Asia, they would be killed!

"Shendu's palace is located near Hong Kong," Uncle said. "He will go there to take his revenge."

"When, Uncle?" Jackie asked.

"At the stroke of midnight," Uncle replied. "On the Chinese New Year."

"That only gives us a couple of

days," Captain Black said.

Jackie shook his head. "Less than that. Hong Kong is sixteen hours ahead of us."

"We'll take Section Thirteen's fastest transport," Captain Black promised. He turned to go.

But Uncle stopped him. "Finding a demon is not enough," he said. "You must know how to defeat it." He stretched, trying to grab a book on a high shelf. It was out of his reach.

Tohru stepped over to get the book. He gave it to Uncle.

"Thank you," Uncle said to Tohru. He turned back to Captain Black. "So I will come with you."

"I will come, too," Tohru grunted.

"Um, that's okay, Tohru," Jackie said.

He still didn't trust the giant.

"Tohru, why would *you* help *us?*" Captain Black asked.

Tohru touched his bandages. Jackie knew that Tohru was angry. Shendu had almost killed the mighty enforcer. And Valmont had never been very nice to him, either.

But all Tohru said was, "I am told Section Thirteen has doughnuts on Thursdays."

Jade laughed. Jackie did, too. He never knew Tohru had a sense of humor!

"You must stay here," Uncle said to Tohru.

"I insist on coming," Tohru said.

"Come here," Uncle said. "I want to tell you a secret."

Tohru leaned down close to Uncle.

With two fingers, Uncle flicked Tohru across the forehead. *Thwap!*

"Ow!" Tohru rubbed his brow.

"You stay here!" Uncle ordered. "Someone must watch the shop!"

Tohru blinked. He would not disobey Uncle.

"Good," Uncle said. "Now, let me gather some important things."

"All right!" Jade cheered. "Let's go save some lives!"

"Oh, no, you don't," Jackie said.

"But, Jackie . . ." Jade pleaded a little while later. "I have to come! I'm an important part of the J-team—the cunning one!"

Jade paced the floor. Jackie and

Uncle were leaving for Hong Kong. She couldn't believe they were going to make her stay home! They were even locking her inside Section Thirteen—with guards to watch her!

"Jade, this is not a movie," Jackie said. "You *know* this time it's too dangerous for you to come along."

Jade sighed. She gazed at a picture of herself with her parents. How could she stay home when her mom and dad were in danger?

"Your mother and father will be safe," Jackie promised her. "I will see to it."

"And I will see to it that *he* sees to it!" Uncle added.

"Be good, Jade," Jackie said. He and Uncle left the room and locked the door behind them. Two guards stood outside. Jade heard Jackie talking to them through the door.

"Don't let Jade fool you," Jackie warned the two guards. "She is very cunning."

That's right, Jade thought. I'm smart. I'm not going to let a few guards stop me from getting out of here!

She waited until she knew Jackie and Uncle were gone. Then her plan began.

She ran to the door and moaned, "Oh, help! My stomach! It hurts! I ate some bad chicken!"

She waited for the guards to open the door. But one of them said, "That's funny. I had chicken for lunch, too. And I feel fine."

Jade frowned. She paced the floor. That didn't work. Time for Plan B. The only trouble was, she didn't have a Plan B.

"It isn't fair!" Jade grumbled. "I'm a prisoner while Jackie's halfway across the ocean."

Her eye fell on the sink in the bathroom. Aha! Ocean. Water. That gave her an idea. . . .

"Oh, guard," Valmont called. He and The Dark Hand enforcers were locked in a cell in another part of Section Thirteen. "Tell me, why haven't we seen Captain Black lately? I miss him so."

"Captain Black went to Hong

Kong," the guard told him. "To find that freak you were working for."

"I see." Valmont nodded. So, he thought. Shendu's treasure is in Hong Kong.

Nothing could stop Valmont from getting that treasure. Not armed guards. Not steel bars. Nothing.

Valmont reached into his mouth and yanked out one of his back teeth.

"Whoa, Big V!" Finn cried. "What are you doing?"

"You'll see," Valmont promised. The tooth was really a remote control. Valmont knew that his cane lay on a table somewhere in Section Thirteen. The cane had a powerful laser beam and an electric sword.

Valmont pushed a button on the

tooth, and the cane rose into the air. It flew through the halls of Section Thirteen. It rounded a corner, on its way toward Valmont's cell.

The guard didn't see the cane coming—until it was too late. He turned, and *thud!* The cane whacked him in the head. The guard fell to the floor.

The cane flew into Valmont's hand. "Perfect," he said. He pulled out the electric dagger. He sliced the dagger through the lock on his cell. The door opened.

"Let's go, boys," Valmont said to his partners. "Shendu's treasure is waiting for us—in Hong Kong."

Chapter 10

The two guards burst into Jade's room. "What's going on here?" they shouted.

Water was pouring out of the bathroom sink and covering the floor. The guards waded through it. It was up to their knees!

Jade giggled as she watched them. She was hiding on a ledge on top of a closet. The closet door was slightly open.

One guard hurried into the bathroom to turn off the water.

Jade pulled a string.

Bang! The bathroom door closed. The guard was locked in!

The other guard ran into the closet, clearly thinking he saw Jade hiding in there. He grabbed something. "Gotcha!"

He thought it was Jade. But it was just a dummy made out of pillows!

Jade jumped from the top of the closet and slammed the door behind her.

"Hey!" the guard shouted. "Let me out!" But he was stuck inside.

"Free at last!" Jade said. She hurried out of the room.

Suddenly, alarms blared. Jade

ducked around a corner. Agents ran past her down the hall.

Whoa, Jade thought nervously. Jackie was serious about my not going to Hong Kong!

Two more agents ran by. Jade heard one of them say, "Valmont escaped. Seal all the exits!"

Jade heard some shuffling in the air vent beside her.

Hmm, she thought. I wonder . . .

She took the grill off the vent and climbed inside. Up ahead of her were Valmont and his thugs.

They were trying to escape through the vent!

Quietly, Jade crawled after them. She stayed a safe distance behind so they wouldn't notice her.

"We're going to Treasure Island," Finn said.

"Treasure Island, *Hong Kong*," Ratso added.

An hour later, Valmont and his men sat in The Dark Hand's private jet. The jet zoomed toward Hong Kong.

They didn't know they had a stowaway. Down below, in the baggage hold of the jet, sat Jade.

She wrapped herself in a warm blanket and turned on a flashlight. She stared at a small picture of her mother and father.

"I've got to save them," she whispered. "I've *got* to!"

"Why haven't we found the palace yet?" Captain Black asked. "It's almost midnight."

"We'll find it," Jackie promised.

Uncle led Jackie, Captain Black, and a team of Section Thirteen agents up a steep hill outside Hong Kong. Jackie could see the lights of the city in the distance. He knew that people were lining the streets, cheering for the New Year.

They reached the top of the hill. "Hot cha!" Uncle shouted. "There it is!" He pointed down below to a flat, empty plain. There was no sign of a palace.

"Where?" Captain Black asked.

"Here," Uncle insisted. "My ancient book does not lie."

"Not even a little?" Captain Black asked.

Uncle frowned. Suddenly, the ground began to shake beneath their feet.

"What's that?" one agent cried.

"Earthquake!" shouted another.

The flat plain below cracked open. A gigantic golden palace burst up from underground. Its towers glinted in the moonlight.

Jackie had never seen such an impressive palace.

Captain Black gasped.

"Never question the ancient book," Uncle told him.

Then something shrieked overhead.

Jackie looked up. A huge shadow passed over them, like a plane or a gigantic bird.

But it wasn't a bird.

It was Shendu.

Shendu flew to the palace and landed in the courtyard.

Jackie and the others perched on the hillside, watching. Shendu didn't see them.

Shendu lifted a claw and tore at the air in front of him. He made a hole in the air the size of a golf ball. An eerie light shot out of the hole.

"What is he doing, Uncle?" Jackie asked.

"He is opening the portal," Uncle said. "To release the dragons."

The small hole slowly began to grow. Jackie stared. Through the smoky light, he saw evil-looking dragons. Hundreds and hundreds of them! They were trying to push their way through the portal—and into this world!

"We can't let those dragons escape," Jackie said. "If we do, we're finished!"

Chapter 11

The portal kept growing. It was now the size of a basketball.

Captain Black motioned to his team of agents. "Let's turn up the heat," he said.

They aimed their high-tech bomb launchers at Shendu.

"No!" Uncle stepped in front of them. "Shendu is immortal. He cannot be killed." Uncle pulled a bottle from his pocket. Inside was a glowing green liquid. "Magic must defeat magic," he said.

Captain Black looked at Jackie.

"He is right," Jackie said.

The agents lowered their weapons.

Uncle waved the bottle at Jackie. "With this balm, you can poke through Shendu's demon shell," he explained. "The talismans are inside him, under his skin. You will be able to reach in and take them."

"All twelve?" Jackie asked.

Uncle shook his head. "You only need a few. But you must choose the right ones." He popped the cork off the bottle. Then he rubbed some of the liquid on Jackie's hands.

"Some of the talismans give Shendu firepower," Uncle said. "But others help his powers to work. For example, the rat talisman gives him life. Without it, he will go back to being a statue."

Jackie stared at his hands. They glowed bright green.

"Be careful, Jackie," Captain Black said.

Jackie hurried down the hillside. He leaped to the top of the palace wall. From there he could see Shendu.

The portal was growing bigger. On the other side, the dragons roared.

"Soon, my warriors," Shendu said to the dragons. "Midnight draws near. . . ."

Jackie sneaked up behind Shendu.

He reached his glowing hands into Shendu's back. He felt around until he touched a talisman.

Startled, Shendu spun around. He knocked Jackie away with a huge claw.

Jackie tumbled across the courtyard.

"You again!" Shendu roared. "How many lives do you have?"

Jackie looked at the talisman in his hand. The dragon. "Excellent!" he cried. "The dragon gives me firepower!"

Jackie aimed the dragon talisman at Shendu. A ray of fire blasted the demon. It blew him across the court-yard.

Thud! Shendu hit a wall and slumped against it. The ray had made a huge hole in his chest.

Wow. That was really easy. Jackie thought. But then the hole suddenly closed up.

Shendu stood up and roared. "You cannot harm me, Chan," Shendu said. "The horse talisman heals me."

In a blur, he sped across the courtyard and knocked Jackie to the ground.

"Umpf!" Jackie groaned. "And the rabbit talisman gives you speed," he said. He rose to his feet. The portal was now so big a man could walk through it. A dragon stuck his huge snout through the hole and roared at Jackie!

"Aaagh!" Jackie yelled. The portal was still too small for the dragons to get through. But it was getting bigger every second. Soon these terrible monsters would be released into the world.

And Jackie wasn't sure he could stop it from happening.

Chapter 12

"At last," Valmont said. "Shendu's palace."

The Dark Hand's jet had just landed outside the huge fortress. Valmont led his enforcers inside. Jade sneaked out of the baggage hold. She tiptoed after them like a spy.

Valmont kicked open a door and gasped. The lost treasure! Huge piles of glittering treasure were stacked to the ceiling!

"Okay. Let's get busy, boys," Valmont said.

The enforcers whooped as they filled their pockets with gold, silver, and gems.

"Chan will keep Godzilla busy out there," Finn said, "while *we* grab the loot!"

Jade left The Dark Hand and peeked into the courtyard. There was Jackie—fighting Shendu!

Jackie reached through Shendu's skin and pulled out a talisman.

"Monkey?" Jackie cried when he saw it. "I was hoping for rabbit!"

He fired the monkey talisman at Shendu—and the demon turned into a bunny rabbit!

"Cute," Jackie joked.

But the Shendu rabbit was no Easter bunny. His eyes glowed red. He blasted heat beams at Jackie.

Jackie ducked and rolled along the ground. When he stood up, the rabbit was gone.

Jackie looked around. "Oh, no," he gasped. "He's invisible!"

The monkey talisman seemed to shoot out of Jackie's hand by itself. But then Shendu the rabbit appeared— with the monkey talisman in its mouth.

Shendu used it to turn back into his old, ugly, demon self.

"Monkey see, monkey do!" Shendu roared. He blasted a heat beam at Jackie.

Jackie dodged it. The beam hit a

statue on the palace wall. The statue turned into the shape of a monkey!

Jackie rolled past Shendu. He plucked a talisman out of the demon's leg.

Shendu turned to blast him.

Jackie kicked him—and Shendu flew across the courtyard.

Jackie glanced at the talisman in his hand.

Jade looked over Jackie's shoulder. "The ox!" she cried. "Good one! That gives you super-strength!"

Jackie wheeled around in surprise. "Jade! How did you get here?"

Jade looked at Jackie's glowing hands. "How did you get your hands all green and—"

Before she could finish, Shendu

lunged at Jackie and grabbed him.

"Talk later!" Jackie shouted.

Jackie struggled as Shendu held him in a tight grip. Shendu turned Jackie upside down and shook him.

The talismans fell out of his pocket. So did the bottle of green liquid Uncle had given him.

It rolled along the ground, stopping at Jade's feet.

Jade picked up the bottle. The green liquid glowed, just like Jackie's hands. She rubbed the liquid on her hands. Now she could help Jackie get back the talismans!

Shendu dangled Jackie in front of the portal. It was now ten feet high. Dragons pressed against it, waiting to come out.

"It is a pity you will not live to see me rule over your world," Shendu said to Jackie. "But you *will* be visiting the *next* world—very soon."

"Heee-yah!" Jade shouted. She flew at Shendu, her hands glowing. She reached inside him, searching for talismans.

Shendu was so surprised that he dropped Jackie.

Jade pulled out a talisman. "A dog!" she cried.

Jackie reached in, too. "I've got the rat! Jackpot! The rat makes statues come to life!"

"Noooo!" Shendu roared. With a mighty crack of thunder, Shendu turned back into a statue. The dragon portal closed up and was gone.

"I will have my revenge," the statue vowed. "If it takes another nine hundred years!"

Jade and Jackie stared at him.

"Hmm," Jade said. "Without the rat talisman, you're just a statue. And without the dog, you're not immortal. You can be destroyed!"

She aimed the dragon talisman at Shendu and blasted him. *Ka-pow!* The Shendu statue blew up into a million pieces!

Jade grinned at Jackie. "Gimme five!"

But the ground began to shake, hard. The palace creaked and groaned.

"It's caving in!" Jackie shouted. "Let's get out of here!" He grabbed Jade and ran off with her.

Jade saw Valmont and his men

through a window. Their arms were full of treasure. But as the palace shook, the treasure turned to sand!

"No, no, no!" Valmont cried. The enforcers grabbed him and dragged him out of the treasure room.

Seconds later, the room caved in.

Jackie and Jade raced up the hillside to join Uncle, Captain Black, and the Section Thirteen agents. They all watched as Shendu's palace was swallowed up into the ground.

Soon the shaking stopped. Nothing was left but the flat, empty plain.

Boom! In the distance, fireworks lit up the city. It was midnight. The Chinese New Year had come, and the world was saved.

"Happy New Year, Jade," Jackie

said. "Happy New Year, Uncle—ow!"

Uncle rapped Jackie on the forehead. "You destroyed the demon!" he cried. "Now the world is out of balance! Yin and yang! Nobody told you to destroy the demon!"

"Jade did it," Jackie explained.

"She is *your* niece!" Uncle shouted. "You are responsible!" He threw his arms into the air and walked away. "Now there is a void," he warned. "A new, *stronger* evil will fill it!"

Jackie sighed. He noticed Jade staring at the fireworks over Hong Kong. He knew she was thinking about home.

"You should visit your parents," Jackie said. "They will be glad to see you."

Jade nodded. "They might want me to stay in Hong Kong with them," she said.

"Would that be so awful?" Jackie asked.

Tears welled up in Jade's eyes. She wanted to hide them from Jackie, but she couldn't. "Awful for *you*," she tried to joke. But it just wasn't funny.

Down on the empty plain, something stirred. Finn, Ratso, and Chow popped their heads out of the ground. Finn spit dirt out of his mouth. Ratso and Chow pulled Valmont up.

"I know how much the treasure meant to you, Valmont," Finn said. "But how about a consolation prize?"

He pointed to a small pile of stones lying in the dirt. The talismans!

Valmont grinned. "They might come in handy one day," he said. "One day very soon . . ."

Chapter 13

"Uncle! I'm home!" Jackie called. He walked into Uncle's Rare Finds. He carried his suitcase in one hand and a dusty statue in the other.

Several months had passed since the Chinese New Year. Jade had stayed in Hong Kong with her parents. Jackie knew his apartment at Section Thirteen would feel empty without her. So he had been off on a dig all this time, searching for ancient treasures.

"Uncle!" he called out again.

"Come, Jackie," Uncle said. "Give Tohru a hug!"

Jackie walked into Uncle's library. Tohru stood beside Uncle, wearing an apron. Jackie eyed him. The last thing he wanted to do was hug Tohru.

"Don't," Tohru said.

Jackie was relieved. "This will take some getting used to," he admitted. "Having Tohru around—and not Jade."

Tohru sighed. "I know."

Uncle picked up a letter off his desk. He waved it at Jackie.

"Ah, that reminds me!" he said. "A letter from Jade's parents arrived yesterday." He read it and said, "They are very pleased with how much she has learned in America."

Jackie smiled. Teaching Jade was not easy—but it was fun.

"One more thing," Uncle added. He stared at the front door of the shop.

Jackie turned to see what Uncle was looking at.

There stood Jade! Her arms were loaded with suitcases. She grinned.

"My parents want me to come back for another year!" Jade shouted. She ran to Jackie and slammed into him so hard, he nearly fell over.

"Jade!" Jackie cried. He was so happy to see her!

Uncle and Tohru gathered around to hug her, too. Shendu was gone, and Jade was back! And everything was right with the world—for now!

Jackie's Big Adventure Word Search

Help Jackie figure out the ancient Chinese secret to long life! In the word puzzle on the next page, find and circle all the words listed below. Look up, down, forward, backward, and diagonally.

TALISMAN	UNCLE
SHENDU	JADE
JACKIE	DRAGON
THE DARK HAND	TOHRU
EVIL	POWER
YIN	FINN
YANG	MAGIC
POTION	ADVENTURE
ARCHAEOLOGY	RATSO
CHINA	ASIA
ZODIAC	CHOW
VALMONT	LUCK

E D A J T A L I S M A N Y
D O U M A N I H C I G A M
R U N I Y A N G S A A T D
A U D N E H S E A R D V N
G O T Y U N C L E C V A H
O S O F T U E C N H E L H
N T R O I I V H O A N M K
K A H E K N C O I E T O R
C R G C E A N W T O U N A
U T A S I A A B O L R T D
L J L D E S E V P O E E E
R Y O S P O W E R G I N H
G Z L E V I L E D Y A Y T

Now, look at the puzzle and find all the letters you didn't circle. Going row by row, write down the uncircled letters on the lines below to uncover the ancient Chinese secret to long life.

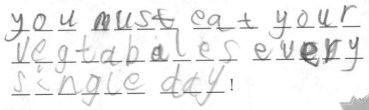

you must eat your vegtabales every single day !

Jackie's A-Maze-ing Maze

Only *you* can help Jackie find his way to the hidden treasure. Complete the maze below.

START

FINISH

Answer on page 122

Jackie's Magic Number Puzzle

Jackie's mission is to find the twelve ancient talismans. In this puzzle every row must add up to 12. Write the numbers 1,2,3,4,5,6, and 7 inside the squares so that each row of three squares adds up to 12. Use each number only once.

Add up the rows across, up and down, and diagonally. There is more than one correct answer to this puzzle.

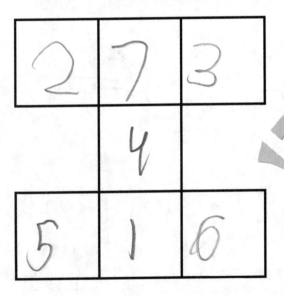

Answer on page 122

Jackie's Talisman Teaser

These two pictures may look alike, but they're not.
Can you find five ways that they're different?

Answer on page 123

Jackie's Secret Message Puzzle

Jackie's got a message for you! Solve this puzzle to find out what it is!

Use the clues to fill in the spaces in Part One. Then match the number under each letter in Part One to the number under each space in Part Two. When you've made a match, write the letter in the space. (See the example we've done to get you started.)

Part One:

1. This talisman gives you the ability to change things into animals.

<u>M</u> <u>o</u> <u>n</u> <u>k</u> <u>e</u> <u>y</u>
2   1

2. What is the name of Jackie's niece?

<u>J</u> <u>a</u> <u>d</u> <u>e</u>
   3   4

3. Which member of The Dark Hand becomes friends with Jackie?

<u>T</u> <u>o</u> <u>h</u> <u>r</u> <u>u</u>
5 6

4. This spirit is the real leader of The Dark Hand.

<u>S</u> <u>h</u> <u>e</u> <u>n</u> <u>d</u> <u>u</u>
7   8 9

5. Where did Jackie find the very first talisman?

bavaria
　　　　10　11

6. The sheep talisman turns you into one of these.

ghost
12　13

7. How old is Jade?

eleven
　　　　14

Part Two:

Write Jackie's message here:

your Mind is
1　6　9　10　2　11　14　8　11　7

your greatest
1　6　9　10　12　10　4　3　5　4　7　5

strength!
7　5　10　4　14　12　5　13

Jackie's Cool Crossword

How much do you know about Jackie and his adventures? See if you can complete the crossword puzzle below.

Across:

2. What kind of store does Uncle own?

5. The name of the agency Jackie works for is called _Section_ 13.

6. Who is Tohru's boss?

8. What are Shendu's warrior ninjas called?

Down:

1. Who always says "One more thing?"

3. How many signs are there in the Chinese zodiac?

4. Where do Jade's parents live?

7. Jackie's boss is named Captain _____.

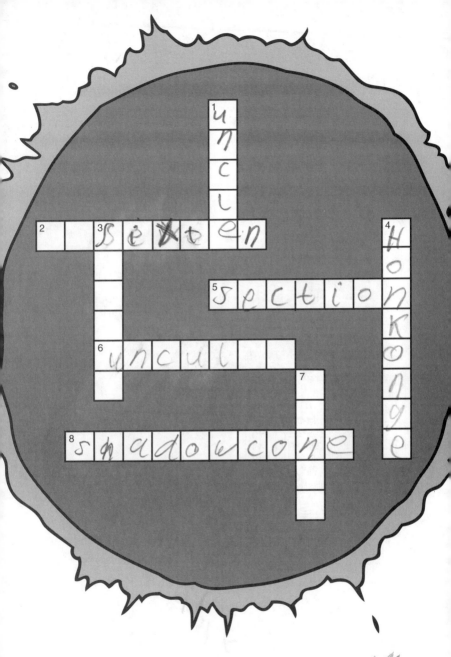

ANSWERS:

p. 113 Jackie's Big Adventure Word Search

You must eat your vegetables every single day!

p. 114 Jackie's A-Mazing Maze

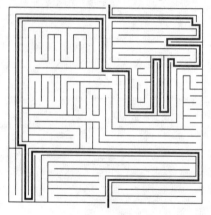

p. 115 Jackie's Magic Number Puzzle

One possible answer is:

2	7	3
	4	
5	1	6

p. 116–117 Jackie's Talisman Teaser

p. 118–119 Jackie's Secret Message Puzzle

1. Monkey
2. Jade
3. Tohru
4. Shendu
5. Bavaria
6. Ghost
7. Eleven

Jackie's message: Your mind is your greatest strength!

p. 120–121
Jackie's Cool Crossword

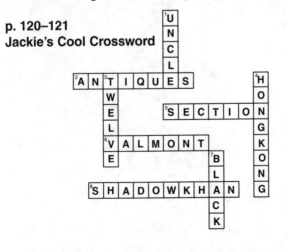

Find out what happens in the next book!

#12 **The Strongest Evil**

Jackie thinks he destroyed the evil spirit of Shendu. But Shendu is back—and he's about to release seven deadly sorcerers into the world!